THE USBORNE BOOK OF
ANIMAL JOKES

written and compiled by
Philip Hawthorn
Designed by Russell Punter
Illustrated by Kim Blundell

What's white and jumps every few seconds?

A polar bear with hiccups.

Turn over the page to find out.

First published in 1991 by Usborne Publishing Ltd, Usborne House, 83-85 Saffron Hill, London EC1N 8RT, England. Copyright © 1991 Usborne Publishing Ltd. The name Usborne and the device ⬚ are Trade Marks of Usborne Publishing Ltd.
Printed in Belgium

WHAT'S THIS?

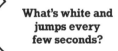

WAY OUT →

What do you call a large, angry sea-bird?
An alba-cross.

If a swan sings a swan song, what does a cygnet sing?
A signature tune.

What should you never do with a 5 ton canary?
Argue.

What lives at the South Pole and smiles?
A pen-grin.

What do you call a failed pelican?
A pelican't.

What's the definition of illegal?
A sick bird.

What bird lives in a refrigerator?
A coldfinch.

Where do storks keep their tins of baked beans?
In a stork-cupboard.

What's yellow, has twenty-two legs and goes crunch?
A canary soccer team eating crisps.

Why should you never tell a secret to a peacock?
Because they're always spreading tails.

Which are the most religious birds?
Birds of prey.

What's white and noisy?
A swan playing the bagpipes.

Where do you go to see seagull paintings?
To an art-gullery.

What's black, flies and does somersaults?
An acro-bat.

Bat-tle

Look, a wing-stand!

LARGE SEA – BIRDS by Albert Ross

What will the cockatoo be on her next birthday?
Cockathree.

What's big, white and Australian, and sits in a tree?
A cooker-burra.

What goes "Hmmm-choo?"
A humming-bird. with a cold.

What's black, white and red all over?
An embarrassed penguin.

What's a bee's favourite bird?
A buzz-ard.

Why did the dinosaur cross the road?
Because chickens didn't exist then.

Why do ostriches have long legs?
So you can tell them apart from strawberries.

What's the grumbliest bird?
A grouse.

An egg-sit.

Why do storks stand on one leg?
Because if they lifted two they'd fall over.

What's yellow and dangerous?
A canary with a hand grenade.

Which bird can lift the heaviest weight?
A crane.

Which seabird was a famous astronomer?
Gullileo.

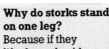
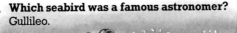
Gull-axy

My tern.

What do you get if you cross…

A homing pigeon with a parrot?
A bird that can ask its way if it gets lost.

A cockerel with a poodle in a Chinese restaurant?
Cock-a-noodle-poodle-doodle-oo.

A cow with a duck?
Cream quackers.

A parrot and whale?
A big blubber mouth.

Q. What do you call an old skunk?

What do you call an anteater who hates ants?
Starving.

Why are camels moody?
Because they've always got the hump.

Heard about the hippy mink?
She was fur out.

What's Australian and calls people names?
A kangar-rude.

What do you call the Australian self-defence expert?
Unarmed Wombat.

What's a polar bear's favourite food?
Iceberg-ers.

What do camels use to wake up in the morning?
A llama clock.

Who's the best known animal in Canada?
Fam-moose.

What's stripey and comes in packs?
Wolves in pyjamas.

Why is a crocodile like a photographer?
They both snap.

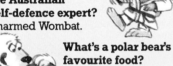

What do you get if you cross...

A snake and a spider?
A cobra-web.

An eskimo with a lizard?
An igloo-ana.

A snake with a clown?
Hiss-terical.

An alligator with a chocolate bar?
Chocodile.

A kangeroo and a bear?
A fur coat with pockets.

A cow and a camel?
Lumpy milkshakes.

An aligator with an apple?
Something that bites you first.

A parrot and a hyena?
An animal that laughs at its own jokes.

A crocodile and a rose?
I don't know, but don't try and smell it.

A skunk with a hedgehog?
A porcupong.

A beaver and an eskimo's house?
Something to ig-gnaw.

Why did the snake have a calculator?
It was an adder.

> I do long division.

What do you call an indecisive snake?
A slithery ditherer.

What's a snake's favourite game?
Hiss-chase.

What snake is always fighting?
A battlesnake.

What's a snake's favourite food?
Slither and bacon.

> I thought it was cherry pie-thon.

What do they sing in the desert at Christmas?
O camel ye faithful.

How do you stop a skunk from smelling?
Hold its nose.

What's got big teeth and annoys people?
An agitator-gator.

What kind of fur do you get from a skunk?
As fur as possible.

> A duck changing its mind.

> Moose is Scottish for mouse.

> Mum, I want to keep my pet skunk under the bed.

> But what about the smell?

> It's OK, he'll get used to it.

> Did you hear about the silly penguin? He took his scarf back as it was too tight.

> I'm boared.

Where do hamsters go on holiday?

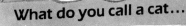

Which mouse was a Roman emperor?
Julius Cheeser.

What's yellow and goes: PPSSSSHHHH!
A canary with a puncture.

What's brown and takes aspirin?
A gerbil with a headache.

What are cold and squeaky?
Mice-icles.

What has yellow hair and pants?
A golden retriever after a long walk.

Why did the dog howl?
Because it saw the tree bark.

What's the difference between...

A crazy rabbit and forged banknote?
One's a mad bunny, and the other is bad money.

An escaped guinea pig and a cold?
It's easy to catch a cold.

HOT DOG by Ken L. Alight

A 3-legged koala climbing a giraffe.

When is a brown dog not a brown dog?
When it's a greyhound.

Why do dogs chase sticks?
To look fetching.

What's the biggest mouse in the world?
A hippopota-mouse.

Have you heard about the dalmation actor?
He's in the spotlight.

What do you call a greyhound covered in custard?
A yellowhound.

What looks like a gorilla and goes "squeak"?
A mouse going to a fancy dress party.

Where do young cats live?
Great Kitten.

What's a scaredy cat?
Something that's pet-rified.

What did the cat say when told it was making too much noise?
Me, 'ow?

What's green and jumps out of aeroplanes with a gun?
A parrot-trooper.

What always follows a dog?
Its tail.

There was a pet rabbit from Gloucester,
Whose owners thought they had lost her.
From the fridge came a sound
At last she was found!
The trouble was, how to defrost her.

What do you call a cat...

That steals things?
A cat burglar.

That's got eight legs?
Octo-puss.

That has a cold?
Cat-arrh.

That's pretending to be a flag?
Pole-cat.

DUCKTOR DUCKTOR

QUACK IN 5 MINUTES – Ducktor

I feel like a clock.
You're too wound up.

I keep stealing chairs
Don't take a seat.

I think I'm a door knob.
Don't fly off the handle.

Now I think I'm a keyhole.
I'd better look into it.

I think I'm a telephone.
Take these – if they don't help, give me a ring.

What has 12 legs, three tails and can't see?
Three blind mice.

A is for Alsatian
B is for Bird
C is for Cat
D is for Dog

What's this?
An alpha-pet.

6

Q. Why don't goats eat jokes?

What do you call a deer who can see well?
A good eye-deer.

What did the horse say when its lunch vanished?
Hay presto!

Why don't cows close doors?
Because they were born in a barn.

How many sheep make a sweater?
None, sheep can't knit.

Why did the cow eat money?
So she could produce rich milk.

Why did the duckpond shake?
Because there was an earth-quack.

KNOCK! KNOCK! WHO'S THERE?

Ee-aw.
Ee-aw who?
Ee-awta let me in.

What do you get if you cross...

Two deer with an extinct bird?
A doe-doe.

A cow with a snake?
A puff-udder.

A cow with an octopus?
An animal that milks itself.

A bull with a sleeping pill?
A bull-dozer.

What do you call a very clever mare?
An expert in her field.

What food is good for horses and pigs?
Hay-corns.

What do you call a horse that's been all round the world?
A globe-trotter.

Why did the foal cough?
Because it was a little hoarse.

What's got four legs and can see just as well at both ends?
A horse with its eyes closed.

How do you hire a horse?
Make it wear stilts.

Where do sheep go on holiday?
The baa-amas.

Where do lambs like to shop?
Wool-worths.
You can always find a baa-gain.

HORSE TALK by Winnie-Ann Nay

Clothes horse

TRADITIONAL TRANSPORT by ORSON KARTE

What goes 'aab-aab'?
A sheep running backwards?

How do sheep keep warm in winter?
Central bleating.

A stick insect in a fluffy jumper.

My warren's got bugs, Bunny.

What do you get from a sheep who loves karate?
Lamb chops.

8

What do you call a stupid squid?
A squidiot.

What comes after a sea-horse?
A dee-horse.

What's on the sea-bed and made of chocolate?
An oyster egg.

What's the difference between a ton and the ocean?
Weight and sea.

What were the whale's children called?
Blubber and sister.

What whale is quackers?
Moby Duck.

How do baby fish swim?
They do the crawl.

Who ate his victims two by two?
Noah Shark.

How do squid get to work?
On an octobus.

What happened when the stupid turtle washed its shell?
It broke the washing-machine.

What bus crossed the ocean?
Colum-bus.

Where do fish borrow money?
From a loan shark.

What's yellow, full of holes and holds water?
A sponge.

How do you confuse an octopus?
Tell it to count to nine on its fingers.

How can you tell a stupid fish?
It shelters under a bridge when it's raining.

And it wears a plastic mac-kerel.

What goes dot, dot, dash?
Morse cod.

I want to hold your hand, your hand, your hand...

What did the octopus say to her boyfriend?

Why didn't the prawn put anything in the collection tin?
Because it was a little shellfish.

Piano tuna

What can fall on the sea without getting wet?
Your shadow.

What fish leaves footprints on the sea-bed?
A sole.

Have you heard about the Dead Sea?
I didn't even know it was ill.

Fish cake

A stick.

Clam clam

Why did the sea roar?
Wouldn't you if you had lobsters on your bottom?

Where do frogs hang their coats?

What's a hound's favourite dance?
The fox trot.

What has long ears and an engine?
A hare-oplane.

How do hedgehogs play leapfrog?
Very carefully.

What's black and white and goes very fast?
A turbo badger.

What's small, spotted and eats mud?
The lesser spotted mud muncher.

Why did the fox sleep on its back?
To keep its tennis shoes dry.

KNOCK! KNOCK! WHO'S THERE?

A spider.
A spider who?
A spider light on so I know you're in.

Heifer.
Heifer who?
Heifer cow is better than none.

Quacker.
Quacker who?
Quacker nother joke and I'm going.

Weevil.
Weevil who?
Weevil see.

Why was the centipede late for the game of football?
It took her two hours to put on her boots.

What happened when the magician changed a plug?
He changed it into a rabbit.

It was an elec-trick.

What did the squirrel say at the end of its hibernation?
Is it half past March already?

DUCKTOR DUCKTOR

For ten years my brother has thought he was a cow.
Why didn't you bring him to me earlier?
We've saved loads of money on milk.

Will you take my temperature?
Why, I've got one of my own?

What's nice to mice?
A lazy squeak-end.

Which part of a fish weighs the most?
The scales.

Where do beavers keep their money?
In a river bank.

Who's the most famous underwater spy?
James Pond.

Why are fishermen like mad dogs?
They're always wanting a bite.

What goes into the water green and comes out blue?
A frog on a cold day.

What's the best way to catch a fish?
Get someone to throw you one.

What do you call a baby crayfish?
A nipper.

Why did the water smell?
It was a duck ponged.

Duck!

I know I am.

The skeleton of a jellyfish.

MICE NIGHTMARES BY I.C.A. Trapp

COW HORROR FILMS by B. Featers

FROG HOBBIES by Leigh Ping

I've got a person in my throat.

FROG CHAIRS by Lilly Padd

SAFE ROAD CROSSINGS BY Luke Left & Den Wright

Spike one!

Coat of arms

Fox glove

(12)

Deer stalker

Deers talking

Where do you find a spider with no legs? Exactly where you left it.

What can never be made right? A grasshopper's left eye.

Why do bees hum? Because they don't know the words

Why did the fly fly? Because the spider spied 'er.

What's got no teeth and lives in a brick? A stupid woodworm.

What's green and hairy and shouts 'Help!'? A caterpillar in a pond.

Why do swallows fly south for the winter? Because it's too far to walk.

Why did the bird sleep under the car? To catch the oily worm.

What did the crow say when it laid a square egg? Ouch!

Which is the sweetest bird on the pond? A coot.

What did the ram say to his girlfriend? I love ewe.

What do you call a young sheep that works in a bar? A baa-lamb.

Why did the one-armed farmer limp into his burning house? To rescue his lucky horseshoe.

When is a cow like a chef? When it's calving.

What do cows do after an earthquake? Produce milk shakes.

I love Moo-zart.

Why did the cow play the violin during milking? She was a moo-sician.

Why did the farmer run a herd of cows over her field? She wanted mashed potatoes.

Why don't rabbits buy holes? Because they can always burrow them.

What do you call a rabbit that works in a barbers? A hare-dresser.

How do you stop rabbits digging up your garden? Hide the spade.

What does an overweight rabbit do when it rains? Gets wet.

Bunion

When is a toad the happiest? In a leap year.

Where do frogs fly their flags? On tadpoles.

I like hop scotch.

What's a rabbit's favourite place? A bun-fair.

I love the mole-er coaster!

Can Caterpillar come out to play?

No, she's just changing.

What are spiders' webs no good for? Flies.

Why was the spider on television? She read the webber forecast.

What game do flies hate most? Squash.

What has fifty legs but can't walk? Half a centipede.

A. In the croakroom.

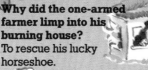

WHAT'S THIS?

13

Q. Why was the baby lion camping?

What's big and grey and looked at by millions?
A tele-phant.

Why is a lion in the desert like Father Christmas?
Because he's sandy claws.

What's the tallest animal in the world?
A flea on a giraffe's head.

What's Greek and swings through the trees?
A monk-kebab.

What animal falls from the clouds?
Rain-deer.

Why does a bear have a fur coat?
Because he'd look silly in a raincoat.

What do you get if you cross…

Hollywood and a tiger?
Stars and stripes.

A hot dog and a fierce wolf?
A fang-furter.

A monkey and the ocean?
A chimpan-sea.

A large monkey with a bell?
Ding-dong King Kong.

Santa's sleigh with a sewer?
Drain-deer.

An elephant with Superman?
Someone who performs difficult tusks.

A bullfrog with a rhino?
A frog-horn.

What's invisible and smells like a banana?
A monkey's burp.

Where do you hang your clothes on safari?
On a clothes-lion

What do you call a giant gorilla with a cement mixer?
King Kong-crete

Which of the apes is the clumsiest?
The orang-utangle.

What do you call a gossipy monkey?
A blab-oon.

What smells and travels swiftly across the plain?
A cheetah's nose.

What monkey is always exploding?
A ba-BOOM!

Why are you scratching yourself?
No-one else knows where I itch.

What cats are like a chain?
Lynx.

THE IGUANA'S LUNCH BY Liz R. Deeting

A CRUSH ON SNAKES BY Anna Conder

SMALL SNACKS BY Anne Teeter

The Drowning Moose by L.Koverbord

SAFARI BY L.E. Phant

A walrush.

Will you remember me tomorrow?
Yes.

Will you remember me next week?
Of course I will.

Knock, knock
Who's there?

You've forgotten me already.

14

What's black and red and noisy?
A ladybird with a trumpet.

What do you call an astronaut fly?
A high-flier.

Heard about the silly leech?
He was no sucker.

Why did the wasp go on the stage?
She wanted to be in show bzzz-ness.

What flies, has stripes, and is very clumsy?
A fumble-bee.

What's the world's largest moth?
A mam-moth.

Why couldn't the butterfly go to the dance?
Because it was a moth-ball.

Why does a butterfly Always do a flutter-by?

What lives in a supermarket and jumps over shelves?
A grass-shopper.

What did the bishop say when she saw a fly?
Let us spray.

Why is a pair of trousers like an old bag of rubbish?
They've both got flies.

What do you call a very cold flea?
Flea-zing.

Why did the glow-worm sit in a bucket of water?
You would, too, if your bottom was alight.

What time is it?
Fly past flea.

Locust High-cust

Bee-side

Bee-yond

BUTTERFLY AND THE ARGONAUTS
And other tales from Greek Moth-ology

A BEE'S FAVOURITE FLOWERS
by Dan D. Lyon & Chris-Anne Themum

Book worm

NEWSFLASH

A leech has just joined the local insect football team. The manager said it was good to have some new blood in the side.

NASTY INSECTS by Miss Keeto

Bee-low

Bee-neath

Which ark animals were not in pairs?
The worms who were in apples.

How can you tell which end of a worm is which?
Drop it into a glass of cola, and see which end burps.

What's the definition of a worm?
A naked caterpillar?

A chameleon on a melon.

What's black, white and red?
A red ant on a newspaper.
A beetle on a toadstool.
A ladybird on a snow ball.

What's black and moans?
A beetle with a migraine.

16

Where do swallows do their shopping?
In a swoop-ermarket.

What's yellow and goes at 500 mph?
A canary in a plane.

What's black, white and red all over?
A messy magpie eating tomato soup.

Which bird is always in the kitchen?
A cook-oo.

How do quails get to work?
On the quail-way.

What flies but never goes anywhere?
A flag.

What do you get if you cross...

A homing pigeon with a woodpecker?
A bird that knocks when it arrives.

An owl and a skunk?
A bird that smells but doesn't give a hoot.

What bird likes a joke?
A lark.

What hawk has no wings?
A toma-hawk.

How did the cat catch a bird?
She hung upside down in the garden and made a noise like a peanut.

What bird makes you gulp?
A swallow.

What's got a red breast and a green hat?
Robin Hood.

What pie can fly?
A mag-pie.

What do you call a wren's offspring?
Child-wren.

What do birds of prey use after a bath?
Falcon powder.

KNOCK! KNOCK! WHO'S THERE?

Cook.
Cook who?
That's the first one I've heard this year.

Owls
Owls who?
No, owls hoot.

A flea getting a trans-fur.

Bat, man, & robin

He's raven mad.

What's the biggest difference between a partridge and a pheasant?
The spelling.

Lovely grub!

Caw!

Robin Hood

Finish this proverb: 'A bird in the hand...'
Makes it hard to blow your nose?

Beak-on

Crazy Crows

Crow-bar

Crow-cus

Crow-quet

Crow-mance

Crow-chet

Crow-sette

Why is a royal crow like a frog?
Because it's crow-king.

What do you call an ugly crow?
Crow-tesque.

18

Q. What did the hyena jump over?

Why did the flea live on the dog's chin?
Because he liked a woof over his head.

What's big and hairy, and over 2,000 miles long?
The Ape Wall of China.

What jumps and collects pollen?
A walla-bee.

What's a tiger cub after it's fourteen days old?
Fifteen days old.

Why can't famous leopards lead a quiet life?
Because they are always spotted.

What's pink and slimy and weighs 4 tons?
An inside out elephant.

Where do woodpeckers leave their cars?
In the car bark.

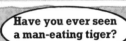

Have you ever seen a man-eating tiger?

No, but I've seen a woman eating yoghurt.

What are you doing?
Just lion around.

A sleepy pigeon looking down a hole.

What do you get if you cross…

A jellyfish with a T.V.?
A jellyfish-on.

A shellfish with a rooster?
Cockle-doodle-do.

A shark with the Loch Ness monster?
Loch jaws.

A whale and a cabbage?
Brussel spouts.

I wish I could spit out of the top of my head.

WHALE HORROR STORIES by R. POON

A fish with a gangster?
The Codfather.

I thought it was a lobster mobster.

A red mullet with a blue shark?
I don't know, but it's purple.

The ocean with a paper boat?
Wet.

A shrimp with a limpet?
A cling prawn.

An icicle with a fierce dog?
Frost bite.

A shellfish with a sheep?
A clam chop.

An oyster with a cat?
A purrl.

A squid with eight cats?
An octo-pus.

FISH SQUASH by Sir Dean Tinn

Why do donkeys go to bed?
Because the bed won't come to them.

What sound do hedgehogs make when they kiss?
Ouch! Ow! Agh!

When are mountain goats most successful?
When they reach their peak.

What's small and squeaks and has a key?
A door-mouse.

What's worse than a giraffe with a sore throat?
A centipede with in-growing toe-nails.

Can you fly faster than a train?
Of course, trains can't fly.

Why couldn't the boy fit an elephant into a match box?
He forgot to take the matches out first.

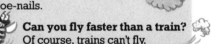

Do you like bison?

I don't know, I've never bised.

Name nine animals from Africa.

Eight elephants and a giraffe.

Hari fishna Angel fish

Goodbye

Keep your big mouth shut and we won't get caught.

Halo.

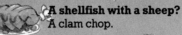

(20)

What's big and ugly and goes "beeep!"?
A monster in a traffic jam.

Why couldn't the caveman sleep?
Because of the dino-snores.

How do you make a shepherd's pie for a monster?
Take three shepherds . . .

What have a car and a mammoth got in common?
They've both got wheels except the mammoth.

What do apes have with their coffee?
A sneezy.

What's the biggest ghost in the world?
An ele-phantom.

I'm reading my horror-scope.

What has six legs, four ears and stripes?
A girl on a zebra.

What has two heads, three horns and five legs?
A buffalo with spare parts.

What's stripy and has 16 wheels?
A zebra on roller skates.

What's black and white and eats like a horse?
A zebra.

Giraffe has a long neck,
So it's said,
To join its body
To its head.

Bee-ver

A.
The low-ena.

What's the difference between...

A buffalo and a bison?
You can't wash in a buffalo.

An elephant and spaghetti?
An elephant doesn't slip off the fork.

A biscuit and an elephant?
You can't dip an elephant in your tea.

An elephant and a pillow?
A pillow never remembers.

An Indian elephant and an African elephant?
About 10,000 kilometres.

WAITER! WAITER!

Do you have chicken legs?
No, I always walk like this.

Do you have wild duck?
No, but I could find a calm one and annoy it for you.

What's this in my soup?
I don't know – all insects look the same to me.

Do they ever change the tablecloths in this restaurant?
I don't know, I've only been here a year.

My plate's wet.
That's the soup.

Will my pizza be long?
No, round.

Restaurant
PERSON NEEDED TO LAY TABLES

What do you call an elephant in the sky?
A thunder cloud.

What monkey is like a flower?
A chimp-pansy.

Where do ant-eaters like to eat?
In a restaur-ant.
MENU

What do you call a deer with no eyes?
No i-dea.

What do you call a deer with no eyes or legs?
Still no i-dea.

What did the tiger say to his girlfriend?
I'm wild about you.

I've a purple nose, three eyes and five green ears – what am I?
Very ugly.

Dad! There's a kangeroo at the door.
Tell him to hop it.

I've just had a bad dream about a horse.
It must have been a night-mare.

What do you get if you cross a brontosaurus with a very old carton of milk?
A dino-sour.

What gets bigger the more you take from it?

My hole.

WHAT'S THIS?
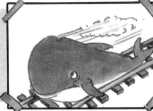

What's got four legs, a shell and fangs?
A terror-pin.

Why was the guinea pig carrying an umbrella?
Because it had forgotten its raincoat.

How did the budgie get to work?
In a budgeri-car.

What's the definition of a toilet?
A jacuzzi for hamsters.

What's brown, flies and wears red underwear?
Super-Gerbil.

What's gold and has a snorkel?
A confused goldfish.

What do you get if you cross…

An alsatian with an oven?
A hot dog.

A labrador with a telephone?
A golden receiver.

A pet dog with a bear?
Winnie-the-Poodle.

DOG'S DINNER BY Nora Bone

THE NAUGHTY KITTEN by Claude Sofa

A whaleway.

Mary had a little cat,
Peter had a pup,
Chrissy had a crocodile
Which ate the others up.

What's yellow and croaks?

What's yellow and smells?

Why did the cat put her kittens in the drawer?

A canary with a cold.

A canary eating garlic

Because you shouldn't leave litter lying around.

What does a Grand Prix cat sound like?

mmeeEEOOooowww!

It runs on pet-rol.

What pets make the most noise?

Trum-pets.

What's grey, buzzes and eats cheese?
A mouse-quito.

What's brown on the top, white on the bottom and goes: "Eeek!"
A mouse sitting on an ice-cube.

What's white and goes round and round?

A mouse in a washing machine.

What's the definition of a cat-flap?
A cat trying to be a bat.

What's the main ingredient in dog biscuits?

I was grey when I went in.

Collie-flour.

woof-les

Watch dog

How did you get on in the milk-drinking contest?

I won by six laps.

What do you call…

A rabbit with its ear in a plug socket?
A current bunny.

A cat that's not house-trained?
Tiddles.

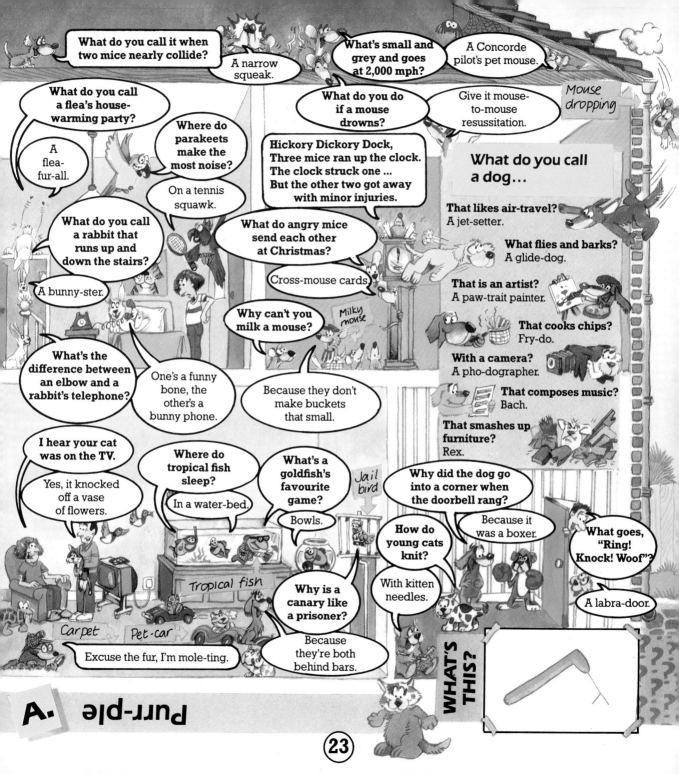

Q. What do piglet gardeners use?

What do you call an Australian chicken?
A kanga-rooster.

What's a horse's favourite game?
Stable tennis.

Where would you find a prehistoric cow?
In a moo-seum.

What's pink and can't keep still?
A pig in a cement mixer.

What do you call a farmer who's full of hay?
Barny.

What do you call a clever duck?
A wise-quack.

A farmer had no chickens. He never bought anything, and no-one ever gave him anything. Yet he had an egg for his breakfast every day. How?
He had ducks.

What's got feathers and crosses valleys?
A via-duck.

Where do cows go on holiday?
Istan-bull.

Duck-chess

What does Farmer Duck drive?
A quack-tor.

Who was the most famous British duck?
Sir Francis Drake.

What do you call a fast duck?
Quack as a flash.

Happy farmily

Eggs-otic

Egg-cited

EGGS-HIBITION

Eggs-pert

Eggs-pensive

£4,000

Where do pigs leave their cars?
On pork-ing meters.

Road hog

Where do pigs go on holiday?
Pen-mark.

I go to Pork-tugal.

What game is played by smelly pigs?
Pig-pong.

What's a pig's favourite ballet?
Swine Lake.

Mine's Sleeping Moo-ty.

Pen and oink.

What does a pig use to write letters?

Why did one pig write to the other?

Because they were pen pals.

What do you call a block of flats for pigs?
A sty-scraper

Mine's the Butt-cracker.

A snake doing press-ups.

What do you get if you cross...

A chicken with a cement mixer?
A brick-layer.

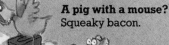

A pig with a mouse?
Squeaky bacon.

A chicken with some wire?
Hen-tangled.

Q. Where do bees like to eat?

Menu

What's small, has
six legs and
breathes fire.
A dragon-fly.

What goes 'bzzzniff'?
A hornet with hay fever.

What do you call
a line of five
mosquitoes?
A mosqui-foot.

Which fly do you find
on a building site?
A crane-fly.

What has lots
of legs and
wears perfume?
A scentipede.

What's the most
timid insect?
Mayfly.

 Bee-ginner

ABC

Gee. What about D,E and F?

BEE-WARE

Bee-stly

Bee-autiful

Bee-fy

Why do bees have
sticky hair?
Because they
have honey combs.

How do bees
get to work?
By buzz.

'Bye buzz!

What do bees say
when they get
in from work?
Honey, I'm home.

What's worse than
being with a fool?
Fooling with a bee.

Where do you put
a crazy snail?
In a nut-shell.

What do you get if
you take away a stick
insect's tea?
A sick insect.

I always eat peas with honey,
I've done it all my life.
It makes the peas taste funny,
But it keeps them on the knife.

What did the
woodworm say when
she saw Pinocchio?
Dinner time!

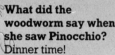

What's got six legs,
a long tongue and
makes pizzas?
A butterfly (I lied
about the pizzas).

What's yellow and
black and speaks
very quietly?
A wasper.

BEE KEEPING by Ivan Ive

What's a worm's
favourite food?
Mud pie.

What marches
round a fort
on 100 legs?
A sentry-pede.

What is a beetle's
favourite pop group?
The Humans.

Why didn't the
woodworm eat the
sofa and armchair?
Because he didn't
like to eat suites
between meals.

How do beetles
tell the time?
With a
clock-roach.

What do you call a
scorpion when it
gets off a rock?
A scorpioff.

A sheep pretending
to be a tree.

INSECTS WITH MANY LEGS by Millie Pede

FROM Caterpillar TO BUTTERFLY by Chris Aliss

BUG HEADGEAR by Anne Tenner

INSECTS

OUTSECTS

Ear-wig go!

Jitterbug

Buggy

Litter bug

26

What lion never roars?

What do you call a hippopotamus with chicken pox?
A hippo-spotty-mus.

What's green and wobbles?
A lizard on a tightrope.

What motorbike does a hyena ride?
A Yama-ha-ha.

How do you hunt bear?
Take your clothes off.

Why don't hippos eat clocks?
It's too time-consuming.

What do you call a puma from Poland?
A pole-cat.

Algy met a bear,
The bear met Algy.
The bear was bulgy,
The bulge was Algy.

Bat-minton

How do you open a monk's door?
With a monk-key.

What are the most expensive animals?
Deer.

How did the animals escape from the shipwreck?
On a gir-raft.

Tie-ger

An ant with bad breath.

What do you get if you cross...

A dinner service with an alligator?
A crockery-dile.

A cheetah with a jet?
I don't know, no-one's ever caught one.

A giraffe and a watchdog?
Something that barks at low-flying aircraft.

A hippopotamus with a potato?
A chippo.

A stupid gorilla and a kangaroo?
A big, thick jumper.

A leopard with firewood?
A cat-a-log.

A fish and two elephants?
Swimming trunks.

A giraffe with a hedgehog?
A long-handled toothbrush.

An elephant with a cup of coffee?
A drink that never forgets.

A bear and a skunk?
Winnie-the-Pooh.

An elephant with a crow?
Broken telegraph poles.

A watchdog and a tiger?
A nervous postman.

An elephant and a light bulb?
A large electricity bill.

An elephant with an encyclopedia?
A big know-all.

A large elk and a fruit?
Strawberry moose.

How do you make an elephant split?
Ice cream, cherries, chocolate sauce, elephant ...

How do you make an elephant sandwich?
First, take a big loaf of bread...

What's the best place buy an elephant?
Jumbo sale.

What do you call a toothless elephant?
Gumbo.

KNOCK! KNOCK! WHO'S THERE?

Lionel.
Lionel who?
Lionel bite you if you don't watch out.

What did the skunk say when the wind changed directions?
Phaw!

What's green and flies?
The jungle in a helicopter.

What do gazelles have that no other animal has?
Baby gazelles.

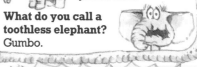

HOW NOT TO MEET LIONS — BY — Claudia Leggov

CLUMSY ELEPHANT by Stan Don McComs

BOUNDING THROUGH THE JUNGLE BY Anne T. Lope

POISONOUS SNAKES by Leigh Thall

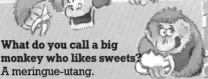

What do you call a big monkey who likes sweets?
A meringue-utang.

What's yellow, then green, then yellow?
A banana working part-time as a cucumber.

What's yellow and points north?
A magnetic banana.

What goes thud, squelch, thud, squelch?
A peanut with one wet shoe.

What's blue and square?
A banana in disguise.

What's the hardest food to eat?
A banana – sideways.

Why are bananas yellow?
So they can hide in custard.

What do monkeys sing at Christmas?
Jungle bells.

What would you rather ate you, a lion or a gorilla?
I'd rather the lion ate the gorilla.

What do you do if a gorilla tells you a joke?
Laugh very loudly.

What deer can you see through?
A win-doe.

Heard about the fireflies who met at sunrise?
It was love at first light.

How do you begin a letter to a stag?
Deer Stag, ...

What plays the trumpet and hisses?
A brass-snake.

Who was the famous monkey general?
Ape-oleon Baboon-aparte.

Why do tigers eat raw meat?
Because they don't know how to cook.

What's the best way to talk to an angry tiger?
Long distance.

What's bright blue and very, very heavy?
An elephant holding its breath.

What's a moose's favourite fruit?
Mooseberries.

What do French geese wear?
Goose-berets.

How do you know when there's an elephant ...

At a barbeque?
He's the one with the biggest ribs.

In your garden?
Peanut shells in the shed.

In your family?
You can never get into the bathroom.

In the custard?
When it's very lumpy.

In the oven?
You can't get the door shut.

What's black, white and red?
A panther eating a strawberry sandwich.

A zebra with a nose bleed.

A sunburnt polar bear with dirty paws.

Hi Ena.

'Ello Phant.

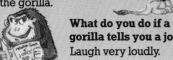

Bad spelling rools O.K

Queen Elizabeth II rules U.K.

Goblin food is bad for the elf....

Esc-ape

FOR THE TEN MILLIONTH TIME— DON'T EXAGGERATE!

Ape-ron

What has a long neck and writes on walls? Giraffiti

People with bad memories are....er.....um..

How do you record an ape?
On an ape recorder.

Rock 'n' mole

A. dandelion.

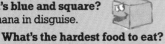

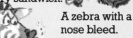

On these two pages are lots of ideas for how you can make up your own jokes about animals, birds, insects, fish and reptiles.

Jokes using animal puns

A pun is when all or part of a word is replaced with a word that sounds like it. For example in this joke:
What do cats like for their birthday?
Purr-fume.
(The first part of the word perfume has been replaced.)

> A pun is sometimes called a play on words.

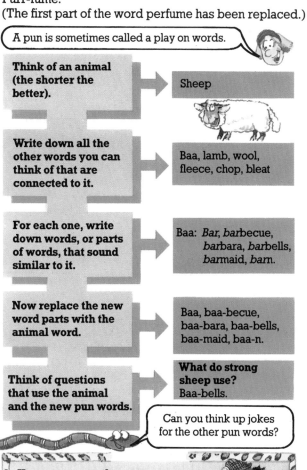

Think of an animal (the shorter the better).
→ Sheep

Write down all the other words you can think of that are connected to it.
→ Baa, lamb, wool, fleece, chop, bleat

For each one, write down words, or parts of words, that sound similar to it.
→ Baa: *Bar*, *bar*becue, *bar*bara, *bar*bells, *bar*maid, *bar*n.

Now replace the new word parts with the animal word.
→ Baa, baa-becue, baa-bara, baa-bells, baa-maid, baa-n.

Think of questions that use the animal and the new pun words.
→ **What do strong sheep use?** Baa-bells.

> Can you think up jokes for the other pun words?

Here are some other pun words for you to try.

Hen-chanted   Bull-garia   Bee-tle
Hen-ergy   Ass-ma   Chimp-ney

Odd animal descriptions

Quite a few jokes in this book use the idea of an animal doing something odd. For example:
What's got eight legs and puffs?
A spider running a marathon.

Write down an animal, and one description of it.
→ Leopard – has spots
Beetle – is black
Dog – goes 'woof'

Write down an everyday object.
→ Calculator
Stilts
Roller skates

Write down what this object would make you do, look like or have.
→ Be good at sums
Be very tall
Have eight wheels

Write your joke using the animal and object descriptions.
→ **What is black and very tall?**
A beetle on stilts.

> Can you complete the last two? You could also swap the animals and objects around.

Here are some more ideas for odd animal jokes. All you have to do is think of the animal and its description.

What's (description) and goes round and round?
A (animal) in a washing machine.

What's . . . and laughs?
A . . . reading a joke book.

What's . . . and glows?
A 100 watt . . .

What's . . . and has stripes?
Sergeant . . .

Types of joke

On this page you can find out some of the different types of animal joke you can make up.

What do you get if you cross . . .

What do you get if you cross a joke book with geese?
A giggle gaggle.

This type of joke is great fun because you can imagine what you get when you cross animals with other things.

A good way of making up these jokes is to do a joke square. There is one below which has been part-filled in. Try and think of things for each blank square.

Don't worry if some of them don't seem to work very well.

Cross these ▶ with these ▼	Leopard	Gorilla	Hippo	Bee
Pot of glue			Stick in the mud	
Computer		A big, hairy know-all		
Jellyfish	Spot the jellyfish			
A rose				A bee-auty

You could try it with different animals and objects.

Obvious jokes

In these jokes, the answer is the most obvious one, which catches the other person out. The most famous example of this joke is:
Why did the chicken cross the road?
To get to the other side.

Below are some jokes for you to complete:

Why did the (animal) wear black shoes?
Because its blue ones were at the menders.

Why do – wear furry boots?
To keep their feet warm.

What's the difference between . . .

What's the difference between a rhino telling jokes and a lettuce?
One's a funny beast, the other's a bunny feast.

There are many types of this joke. The one above uses two words that make sense when the first letters are swapped round. (This is called a spoonerism.)

Cat flap – flat cap   Hiss mystery – miss history

A note on making up jokes

Jokes can come in two ways: easily and with great difficulty. Sometimes a joke seems to drop into your head from nowhere. But most of the time you will need to work hard to make them up.

The thing to remember is: don't give up!

Knock! Waiter! Doctor!

These three types of joke can also include animals. Here are some ideas for each type which you can use to make up more jokes:

Knock! Knock!

Noah (Know a . . .)
Atch (Atch-oo . . .)
Ernie (Any . . .)
William (Will you . . .)
Howard (How would . . .)
Shirley (Surely . . .)
Sarah ('S there a . . .)
Alison (I listen . . .)
Noel (Know all . . .)

Waiter! Waiter!

There's a dead fly in my soup.
What's this fly doing in my soup?
Your sleeve's in my soup.
Do you have frog's legs?

Doctor! Doctor!

I feel run down.
People keep disagreeing with me.
My nose keeps running.
I keep losing my memory.

A. A comedi-hen

Q. How do snail ghosts move?

What does it say on the sign outside the haunted hive?
Bee-ware.

Heard about the dog skeleton?
It was always burying itself.

Why don't dragons like knights?
Because they can't stand tinned food.

What animal was the noisiest sleeper?
A bronto-snoreus.

What does a cow ghost say?
Mooooooooooo!

What do you call a mad sheep?
Baa-my.

KNOCK! KNOCK! WHO'S THERE?

Weirdo.
Weirdo who?
Weirdo you think you've been?

Thumping.
Thumping who?
Thumping with big teeth is climbing up your neck.

Howie.
Howie who?
I'm all right, how are you?

What do you get if you cross…

An angry monster with a pet bird?
A budgeri-grrrrr!

A lion with a graveyard?
The cata-tombs.

A dragon with an insect?
A fire-fly.

Why couldn't the dog act with a ghost?
Because he got stage fright.

Alas, poor ostrich . . .

Are you famous?

I'm a nobody.

Nice cos-tomb.

What did the monster call his pet hippo?
Dinner.

What's grey and covered in feathers?
An elephant standing next to an exploding chicken.

What's white and as tall as a giraffe?
A giraffe ghost.

What swims and makes a ghostly noise?
A whale.

What do you call an Australian ghost?
A kangar-ghoul.

They live in the Northern Terror-tory.

What do wolf ghosts think of dracula films?
Fangtastic.

What's black and white and lives in Scotland?
The Loch Ness Zebra.

What's brown and hairy and goes 'slam, slam, slam, slam'?
A four-door gorilla.

Famous animal last words

A monkey:
Who put grease on the treeeeeeeee!

A fish:
Who pulled out the plug?

A squirrel that thought it was a bird:
It's easy, you just flap your arms and….

A worm:
You're up early..

A woodpecker:
Of course this isn't an exploding tree.

A hedgehog:
What's that rumbling noise?

What time is it when you meet a hungry monster?
Time to run.

Let's fly, flea.

Let's flee, fly.

What tunnels through earth and smells rotten?
Mole-dy.

A. Dead slowly.

32